SCOOBY-DOO!

Case Files #3:

The Scary Scooby

Written by James Gelsey

A
LITTLE APPLE
PAPERBACK

SCHOLASTIC INC.

New York   Toronto   London   Auckland   Sydney
Mexico City   New Delhi   Hong Kong   Buenos Aires

No part of this publication may be reproduced in whole or in part, or stored in a retrieval system, or transmitted in any form or by any means, electronic, mechanical, photocopying, recording, or otherwise, without written permission of the publisher. For information regarding permission, write to Scholastic Inc., Attention: Permissions Department, 557 Broadway, New York, NY 10012.

ISBN-10: 0-439-91594-5

ISBN-13: 978-0-439-91594-6

Copyright © 2007 Hanna-Barbera.

SCOOBY-DOO and all related characters and elements are trademarks of and © Hanna-Barbera.

Published by Scholastic Inc. All rights reserved.

SCHOLASTIC, LITTLE APPLE, and associated logos are trademarks and/or registered trademarks of Scholastic Inc.

Designed by Michael Massen and Two Red Shoes Design

12 11 10 9 8 7 6 5 4 3 2 1   7 8 9 10 11/0

Special thanks to Duendes del Sur for cover and interior illustrations.

Printed in the U.S.A.

First printing, October 2007

Hi! I'm Velma Dinkley, and this is Daphne, Fred, Shaggy, and of course, Scooby-Doo! We're the gang from Mystery, Inc. and we're really glad you could join us. We've just come back from a super-tough case that we think you may be really interested in.

In these pages, we've recorded everything that happened at the scene of the mystery. You'll

find notes, photographs, and even puzzles to help you identify the suspects and connect the clues. When you're done, you'll be on your way to figuring out who's behind the Mystery of the Scary Scooby!

So sharpen your pencil, get out your magnifying glass, and turn the page for your first Case Files Entry. Good luck!

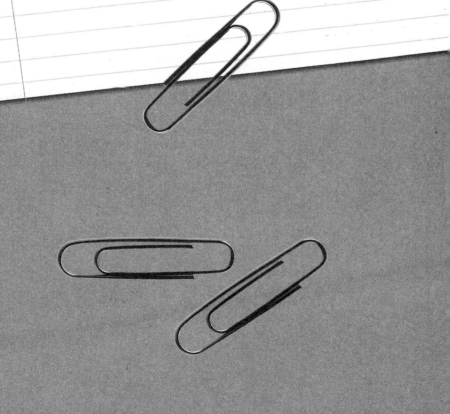

From the desk of
Mystery, Inc.

"Man, I hate w-w-winter!" Shaggy said through chattering teeth. He was huddled in the back of the Mystery Machine trying to stay warm. The heat in the van wasn't working very well, so we were all a little cold. Fred concentrated on the snowy road, while Daphne and I studied an oversized brochure.

"Look at those people sailing!" Daphne said in amazement.

"And playing volleyball," I added. "And surfing!"

"Ah, memories of summer," Shaggy said wistfully. "Remember those days, Scooby-Doo?"

"Reah," Scooby sighed, with a slight nod.

"Shaggy, we're not talking about summer," Daphne said. "We're talking about winter."

"Huh?" Scooby asked.

"Daphne's right," I said. "Look." I held up the brochure for Scooby and Shaggy to see.

"Zoinks!" Shaggy exclaimed. "Like, those people are sailing on a frozen lake. And they're playing volleyball in the snow! And surfing down a mountain!"

I flipped over the brochure to show Shaggy and Scooby the front.

"Winterama Sports Resort. Where there's no business like snow business!" Shaggy read. "Sounds really cool to me."

"I know, doesn't it?" Daphne asked.

A cool adventure awaits us!

"No, like, literally sounds cool, as in bone-chilling cold," Shaggy said, shaking his head. "I mean, doing all those summertime things in the winter? You'd be freezing!"

"Reah, reezing!" Scooby echoed. He wrapped another scarf around his neck and pulled his woolen cap down tighter.

"The resort is owned by Bridget LaNeige," I told them. "She's that skier who won all those gold medals in the past two Winter Olympics."

"And she just bought the Blizzard Diamond," Fred said. "The Blizzard Diamond is one of the most famous and expensive diamonds in the world. Which is why we're really here. Bridget LaNeige called us to explain that she's been getting letters from someone threatening to steal the diamond. We're going to snoop around while we play, so this'll be like a working vacation."

The van whizzed past a large "Welcome to Winterama!" billboard. A giant likeness of Bridget LaNeige smiled down on us.

Fred pulled up in front of the largest log cabin any of us had ever seen. It was really cold, so we all jumped out of the van, grabbed our bags, and ran inside. As soon as we passed through the large revolv-

Shaggy and Scooby always come prepared.

ing door, the warmth of the lobby, which probably came from the fire in the huge stone fireplace, washed over us.

"Now that's more like it!" Shaggy said. "And speaking of s'mores . . . come with me, Scoob."

Shaggy reached into his bag and pulled out a small metal case. He opened the case and removed two skinny metal rods that extended like an antenna and handed them to Scooby. Shaggy then removed a small plastic bag from the case and tore it open with his teeth.

He took out two marshmallows and stuck them on the ends of the metal rods.

"You hold these while I get the rest of the things ready," Shaggy said to Scooby. Scooby began toasting the marshmallows in the fireplace as Shaggy unwrapped the graham crackers and chocolate.

"I never travel anywhere in the winter without my portable s'mores kit," Shaggy said.

When the marshmallows were nicely browned, Shaggy and Scooby quickly removed them from the flames. They sandwiched the marshmallows between the graham crackers and chocolate and gently removed the roasting sticks. Mouths watering, Shaggy and Scooby raised the treats to their lips.

"Man, I love winter!" Shaggy announced.

I won't bore you with any more details of Shaggy and Scooby eating their s'mores, so why don't you check out the next page. You'll find a puzzle that will help you sharpen your detective skills.

Puzzle #1

The words in the list below are hidden in this puzzle. Find them and circle them. Then unscramble the left-over letters to spell out the answer to the bonus question.

BLIZZARD
BOBSLED
BOOTS
CHAIRLIFT
COLD

EARMUFFS
FIREPLACE
GLOVES
HOLIDAY
HOT COCOA

ICE SKATES
JACKET
JANUARY
MUFFLER
SKI

S'MORES
SNOWMAN
TOASTY
WIND

C C T G L O V E S U
H O T C O C O A S
O S L E R D N I W
N L E M D K M O E Y
I T U D U C W C D R
D A F F M A R E A
A K F A L A J L U S
Y S L N P Z B S N M
E E E Z O B A O
A C R I G O J R
T F I L R I A H C B T E
O F B T O A S T Y I K S

BONUS QUESTION: What has no beginning, end, or middle?
(Hint: Shaggy and Scooby enjoy them all year round)
ANSWER: __ __ __ __ __ U __ H __ __ __ __ __ __

From the desk of
Mystery, Inc.

"Just what do you think you're doing?" bellowed a woman in a black pantsuit. She raced across the lobby, hurtling over piles of luggage. "You can't do that here!"

Shaggy and Scooby looked puzzled.

"Like, do what?" Shaggy asked as he took a bite of his s'more.

"Guests are not allowed to cook in the lobby fireplace!" the woman exclaimed.

"They're sorry," Daphne said. "It won't happen again...right, fellas?" She shot Shaggy and Scooby a serious look.

Shaggy and Scooby munched and nodded.

"Oh, it's all right," said a woman sitting by the fireplace. She was wearing a bright red, white, and blue tracksuit with the letters "U.S.A." on the front. As she stood up, we couldn't help but notice the dazzling diamond that hung on a golden rope around her neck. "We want our guests to feel at home here, right, Hun?"

The woman in the black pantsuit nodded.

Hun Strelbing ↑

and ↑
Bridget LaNeige

"Whatever you say, Bridge," she replied in what sounded like an angry voice. "You're the boss."

"I'm Bridget LaNeige, and this is Hun Strelbing, my head of security," said the woman in the tracksuit cheerfully, pointing to the stern woman in black. "You must be the Mystery, Inc. gang. Welcome to Winterama! How are you finding things so far?"

"Relicious!" Scooby said.

"I'm with him," Shaggy added, as he licked the chocolate from his fingers.

"Wonderful!" Bridge LaNeige said. "We have lots of wonderful activities, so you'd better get started if you want to try them all. And don't forget our wonderful evening entertainment. I've brought in Paolo Pegetto, a puppeteer I met during one of my skiing exhibitions in Italy. He's a genius and absolutely wonderful!"

"By the way, Ms. LaNeige, that's a beautiful diamond you're wearing," Daphne said.

"Oh, my, isn't it wonderful?" Bridget said. "I purchased it at an auction last month. It cost me every last cent that I didn't put into the resort. But it was worth it, even with the crazy letters I've been receiving. But that's Hun's worry, not yours. Have a wonderful time, everybody!"

Suddenly, a woman ran up to Bridget LaNeige.

"Oh, Ms. LaNeige! I'm your biggest fan!" The woman was wearing an official "Bridget LaNeige" ski suit. She thrust a copy of SNOW SPORT MONTHLY with Bridget's picture

Brenda, Bridget's creepiest
& biggest fan.

on the cover right under Bridget's nose. "Could you please sign this? Please? Make it out to 'My best friend, Brenda'!"

Bridget smiled warmly and said, "Oh, that's so sweet. Don't you think so, Hun?" I could tell by the look she gave Hun that Bridget was a little uncomfortable. Hun jumped into action.

"Sorry, autographs after dinner," Hun said, coming between Bridget and Brenda the fan. Bridget shrugged as if there was nothing she could do and then walked away.

"But Bridget! Bridget! Just an autograph!" Brenda cried out. Hun finally shooed Brenda, the crazed fan, away. As she walked off, Brenda yelled, "That's no way to treat your biggest fan, Bridget. What goes around, comes around, you'll see!" Sheesh! With fans like that, who needs enemies, I thought. But then suddenly I remembered why Hun Strelbing's name sounded so familiar.

"Weren't you on the Olympic ski team too?" I asked her.

Hun nodded and let out a heavy sigh. She explained how she and Bridget were on the U.S. ski team together. They became roommates and best friends. Hun told us how one morning in their room she had tripped on one of Bridget's shoes and wrenched her knee. Hun couldn't ski, so Bridget was given Hun's slot at the Olympics where she ended up winning a bunch of gold medals.

"We stayed friends, and Bridget earned a ton of money in endorsements and used it to buy and renovate this resort," Hun continued. "She hired me to be her head of security and personal bodyguard."

"She must have managed her money wisely in order to buy this place and that diamond she was wearing," I said.

Hun nodded and said, "That's no ordinary diamond she's wearing." She took a folded piece of paper from her pocket and showed it to us. It was a picture of the same diamond that Bridget was wearing. The words "Anne Tique's Auction House" were written across the top. It was a page from an auction catalog.

"Jeepers! The Blizzard Diamond!" Daphne gasped. "Bridget's wearing the Blizzard Diamond!"

"Shhhhh, not so loud," Hun urged. "I don't want to draw any unnecessary attention to it. And you two . . . no more cooking in the lobby fireplace. And as for the rest of you, watch your step. You can never tell

Entry #2

A page from the auction catalog

how something as silly as tripping over a shoe can change the course of your life forever."

As Hun Strelbing walked away, we couldn't help but feel a little sorry for her.

"So, like, what do we do now?" asked Shaggy.

"I say we hit the snow!" Fred said.

We were at the resort for only a few minutes and we'd already met a couple of very important people. But one of them in particular stood out to us. Unravel this next puzzle to see who we're talking about.

Puzzle #2

The name of our second suspect is written below, but you'll need to use the Velmabet to decode it!

Suspect #1 is: Dtk Rsqaiefkc
For extra credit, decode the suspect's motive:
Rda inrs sda cnim jamvi sn Eqfmcas!

Here's a hint: using the Velmabet,
velma = uaijv

Velmabet ➘

➚ Alphabet

Suspect #1 is:

___ ___ ___

___ ___ ___ ___ ___ ___ ___ ___ ___ ___

Here's how to make your Velmabet decoder:

◎ In the top row of boxes, write the letters V, E, L, M, & A. Then write the rest of the alphabet from A-Z leaving out the letters V, E, L, M, & A. Those letters should appear only once, at the beginning of the Velmabet.

◎ In the boxes below the Velmabet, write the letters of the regular alphabet from A-Z. Remember, when writing both the Velmabet and the alphabet, write from left to right, and use only one letter per box.

◎ To crack the code, swap the letter of the Velmabet with the letter of the alphabet directly below it.

Velmabet

Alphabet

the motive is:

___ ___ ___   ___ ___ ___ ___   ___ ___ ___

___ ___ ___ ___   ___ ___ ___ ___

___ ___ ___   ___ ___ ___ ___ ___ ___

Now that you know we're keeping an eye on Hun Strelbing, Bridget's head of security, why don't you read on to find out some of the other people we met at the Winterama Sports Resort.

From the desk of
Mystery, Inc.

After we put our bags away, we went down to the Winterama Activity Center, also known as the WAC. The WAC was a bustling log cabin behind the lodge. Giant electronic boards flashed information about every single activity at the resort. The WAC was also where you could rent skis, snowboards, and any other equipment you needed for winter sports.

"Jinkies!" I gasped. "This is a very impressive operation. There are tons of people here, yet everything's moving like a—"

"—A precision timepiece," a man's voice said, cutting me off. I turned around to see a bushy mustache poking out from

Gordon
Ticktockery

beneath a heavy fur hat. The little man was swaddled in an overcoat and a digital camera hung around his neck. He raised his left arm and pulled back his coat sleeve. "Just like this antique watch. It's over one hundred years old, but it still keeps time as well as it did on the day it was made. And do you know why?"

"Really strong battery?" Shaggy guessed.

The man "tsked" and said, "No, because every piece is finely calibrated to work with the pieces around it. You can't find craftsmanship like this anymore. Or even a watch like this anymore. If it weren't for the loose winding stem, this watch would be perfect."

The man gazed at his watch for a moment and then put down his arm. We really wanted to get our skis on, but the man kept talking to us.

"I'm Gordon Ticktockery," he said. "Collector of fine antiques — watches, jewels, and such."

"What's with the digital camera?" Fred asked.

The man smiled. "I know, it's not a collector's item, but it really helps me with my work," he said. "When I come across

Entry #3

something I like, I can snap a picture on the spot and then print it out. I always travel with my portable printer."

Gordon Ticktockery looked around and then drew us closer.

"Have you kids seen anything that looks like this?" he whispered. He took a piece of paper from his pocket and showed it to us. It was the same page from the auction catalog that Hun had shown us!

"That's the Blizzard Diamond!" Daphne said rather loudly.

"SHHHHHHHH!" Gordon Ticktockery said, stuffing the photo back into his pocket. "Not so loud."

"I don't get it," Fred said.

Gordon explained that he had been at the auction where the Blizzard Diamond was sold because he desperately wanted it for his collection. He showed us a well-thumbed booklet that he carried in his coat pocket. It was a catalog from Anne Tique's Auction House.

"It would have been the jewel in my crown, so to speak," he said. "The auction room was filled with colleagues of mine. And they all dropped out to watch as Bridget LaNeige kept raising the bids. They sat back and

The not-so-friendly staff at the Winterama Sports Resort

basked in my humiliation as I lost to that spoiled snow queen."

"Mr. Ticktockery! Mr. Ticktockery! Time for your snowboard lesson!" A Winterama staff member in a green "Staff" jacket came over to us. "You missed your three o'clock lesson. I was able to move things around and get you in now," the man said.

"What do you mean? I don't have time for snowboard lessons!" Mr. Ticktockery spat. "Good day!" And with that, he stormed off.

The staff member told us how he'd been teaching Gordon Ticktockery how to snowboard for the past few days. He said that Ms. LaNeige even forced him to use some of his own free time to do it.

"That doesn't seem very fair," Daphne said.

"Unless you were paid extra for it," Fred added.

"Well, I wasn't!" the staff member replied bitterly. "Ms. LaNeige wants all of her V.I.P. guests to be given extra-special care, even at the expense of her staff."

This guy didn't seem to like Bridget very much.

"How about snow volleyball?" Fred asked.

The man smiled and pointed the way.

"Do we really have to go back outside?" Shaggy moaned. "'Cause if we do, I'm afraid my goatee's gonna, like, freeze off!"

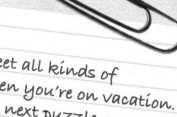

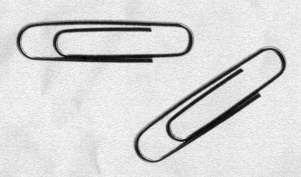

You really do meet all kinds of interesting people when you're on vacation. If you figure out this next puzzle, you'll see which of the people we just met was especially interesting to us.

Entry #3

Puzzle #3

Figure out what letter is different in each pair of words below. Then put that letter in its numbered space to spell out the rest of the letters in the name of the second suspect.

16. REACHES and RESEARCH
12. NOODLE and OLDEN
2. REPEAT and OPERATE
4. WINGED and WEDDING
13. TRACING and RATING
5. SPOOLS and SLOPS
11. PLATTERS and STAPLER
14. NOTE and TOKEN
6. FRIED and FINDER
9. SECRET and RESET
1. SHOT and GHOST
15. WONDER and DROWN
7. WRITING and WIRING
8. PERCH and CIPHER
17. SEA and EASY

Suspect #2 is:

___ ___ R ___ ___ ___
 1   2   4   5   6

___ ___ ___ K ___ ___ ___ ___ ___ ___ ___
 7   8   9   11 12 13 14 15 16 17

So now you know that Gordon Ticktockery is our second suspect. It was easy to forget that just about everyone else at the resort was just there to have a good time. Or so we thought, until we bumped into someone suspicious at the snow volleyball courts. Read on to see what we mean.

From the desk of
Mystery, Inc.

The outdoor snow volleyball courts looked like ordinary volleyball courts, except that the ground was covered with hard packed snow. Most of the players were average athletes, but they were laughing and joking around and having lots of fun. We walked over to a man wearing a green staff jacket.

"Pardon me, we were wondering how we could get into a game?" asked Fred.

The man turned around, looked at Fred, and asked, "Are you talking to me?"

"Yes, we just wanted to know how we can play," Daphne said.

The man shrugged and shook his head. "No idea," he said. "I mean, it's not like I work here or anything."

Wellington
Jeffries

"You don't?" I asked. "But you're wearing a staff jacket."

The man looked down at his jacket and gasped. "Oh, no! I must have picked up the wrong jacket off the bench over there! This is terrible!"

"Was something valuable in your jacket?" asked Daphne.

"My digital camera and some important papers," the man replied. "And a . . . well, never mind. Do you know where the lost and found is?"

"Since it doesn't look like we're going to get in a game, we'll show you the way," Fred offered.

"Thanks," the man said. On the way, he introduced himself as Wellington Jeffries. He told us he had come to the resort to meet with Bridget LaNeige.

"She has my family's diamond," Wellington said. He explained how his grandfather discovered the diamond years ago and named it the Blizzard Diamond because he got caught in a blinding snowstorm right after finding it. Wellington's grandfather loaned it to a museum but then died, so the museum decided to keep it. The museum sold it to a private collector, and the private collector kept it until last month when it was sold at the auction.

"The diamond rightfully belongs in my family," Wellington said, growing increasingly frustrated. He told us how he tried to talk to Bridget, but her giant bodyguard kept shooing him away.

"I even had a replica of the diamond made to give to her in exchange for the real one," Wellington said.

When we got to the lost and found desk, the clerk handed Wellington Jeffries his own green jacket. It did look a lot like the staff jacket. Wellington frantically searched the pockets. He reached into the inside pocket and his hand tore through the lining, popping out through the bottom of the jacket.

"There was a hole in my pocket!" he exclaimed. "They're gone!"

"What's gone?" asked Velma.

"The papers that proved that the diamond really does belong to my family," Wellington said.

In another pocket, Wellington found his digital camera, a page from the Anne Tique's Auction House auction catalog featuring the Blizzard Diamond, and a small fabric pouch

Paolo Pegetto sure
did like Scooby-Doo!

containing the replica diamond.

"This is terrible!" Wellington moaned.

"This is amazing!" another voice shouted at the exact same time.

A short man in black pants, a white shirt, and a brown vest scurried over to us. He stood in front of Scooby, studying his face.

"This face, it is amazing!" the man gasped. He took out a measuring tape and quickly measured the size of Scooby's face. "So expressive. So real. I must have this face!"

"Sorry, but it's like connected to my best friend!" Shaggy interrupted.

The little man chuckled and apologized. "So sorry," he said. "I am Paolo Pegetto, the puppet man. And I would love to use your friend here as a model for a new puppet I would like to use in my show tonight." He looked at us hopefully.

"C'mon, Scoob, you'll be famous!" Shaggy said.

"Would some pictures help?" Wellington suggested. "I can take some shots with my digital camera. And I have my portable printer in my room."

Paolo Pegetto began to smile again. He gave instructions to Wellington Jeffries about the kind of pictures to take. They photographed Scooby from all possible angles while Scooby posed. He appeared to be enjoying himself immensely. But I was curious about one thing: Why would a famous puppet-maker come all the way from Europe just to perform at a glorified ski resort? So I asked Mr. Pegetto.

"Because Signora LaNeige gave my career a big bump," he answered. "I was famous in Europe and she promised me to be famous in the United States. But when I come here, all I see is that I am not famous. Even a little snowy diamond is more famous than Paolo Pegetto. So I live and I learn, but I never forget. Signora LaNeige, she will see what comes of lying to Paolo Pegetto."

And with that, Paolo left with Wellington to print out the pictures he had just taken. The rest of us went to get ready for dinner.

Once again our paths crossed with some memorable characters. But they were memorable for different reasons and only one of them was worth keeping an eye on. Figure out this next puzzle, and you'll see who I'm talking about.

Puzzle #4

Place the words below into the grid, making sure not to leave any empty spaces. When you're done, unscramble the letters in the shaded squares to spell out the last suspect.

HOOD
BOOTS
EARMUFF
SKI MASK
SOCKS

MITTENS
UNDERSHIRT
JACKET
TURTLENECK
PARKA

SCARF
SNOWSHOES
LONG JOHNS

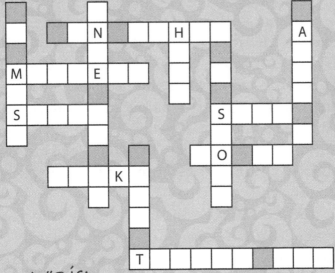

Suspect #3 is:

___ ___ ___ L ___ ___ ___ ___ T ___

___ ___ F ___ ___ ___ ___ E ___

Phew! It sure was a busy afternoon. We discovered that Wellington Jeffries was our third and final suspect. We were looking forward to some R&R at the show that night. Check out what happened. It's something none of us (especially Scooby) ever could have predicted.

From the desk of
Mystery, Inc.

After dinner that night, we went to the Winterama Theater for the show. Bridget LaNeige welcomed everyone. The spotlight on Bridget flashed on the Blizzard Diamond, reflecting a painfully sharp light that made it hard to see.

Bridget introduced Paolo Pegetto and returned to her seat. The houselights went out, plunging us into darkness. We could hear some activity on the stage, and when the stage lights came on, there he was.

Paolo Pegetto stood on the stage beside a tall black curtain about ten feet long. He climbed a stepladder and stood behind the curtain so we could see his upper body. The lower half of the curtain opened, revealing a row of life-size marionettes. The one on the end looked just like Bridget LaNeige. And the one at the far end looked just like Scooby-Doo!

"Hey, look, Scoob, you're on stage!" Shaggy gasped.

Scooby giggled with excitement.

Paolo Pegetto picked up the crossbar with

An innocent puppet show soon turns . . . well, you'll see!

the strings and, with the slightest tug of his hand, brought the Bridget marionette to life. Everyone laughed and clapped as Paolo's Bridget LaNeige marionette reenacted the real Bridget's Olympic skiing career, including her gold medal ceremony. After a short intermission, Paolo put on a show with the rest of the marionettes. He acted out almost everything that had occurred since we arrived at the Winterama Sports Resort that morning.

"Hey, that looks like that Wellington Jeffries guy we met earlier," Fred said.

"And that looks like Bridget's bodyguard," Velma said.

"And there's Scooby getting into trouble!" Shaggy said. In fact, that's exactly what was happening. The Hun Strelbing marionette was scolding the Scooby marionette for making s'mores in the fireplace.

"Boy, that Paolo Pegetto sees everything," Daphne whispered. "It's a little creepy."

The Scooby marionette shoved the Hun Strelbing marionette. The audience laughed, but we didn't.

"Rhat's rot rice!" Scooby exclaimed.

"We know you would never do that, Scooby," Daphne said.

Bad Dog, evil twin Scooby!

The Scooby marionette then turned towards the audience and barked. The audience laughed again. The Scooby marionette walked to the edge of the stage. We could tell that Paolo Pegetto was struggling to control his puppet, but he couldn't — the Scooby puppet jumped right off the stage and onto the real Bridget LaNeige's lap. The audience — including Bridget LaNeige — kept laughing, thinking it was part of the show. But we could tell by Paolo's panicked expression that it wasn't.

The Scooby puppet gave Bridget a big lick on the cheek. Then he jumped off and ran up the aisle and out the theater door. Everyone applauded. But suddenly Bridget LaNeige let out an ear-piercing scream.

"My diamond!" she cried. "That dog stole my diamond! Call the police! Where's my bodyguard? Where's Hun Strelbing? HUN!"

The houselights came on as the audience began to panic. Hun Strelbing ran into the theater.

"Calm down, everybody, calm down!" she said. She ran onto the stage and picked up the microphone. "Take it easy, everyone. It's snowing again, and there's a blizzard warning for the entire area. So no one's going anywhere. Don't worry, Bridget, we'll find the culprit!"

"Look! There's that dog!" someone shouted from behind us. All eyes turned to Scooby.

Scooby swallowed. "Gulp!"

"Shaggy, you take Scooby back to the room!" Fred whispered. "The rest of us will see if we can find anything."

Scooby and Shaggy smiled and waved as they slid out of their seats and left the theater.

The rest of us went to look for clues. Just outside the main theater door, we spotted something. Examine the photograph Fred took. See if you can tell what it was that we saw. Then solve the puzzle on the next page to see if your hunch is correct!

Puzzle #5

Unscramble these words having to do with winter and then put the numbered letters in the correct order to spell out the clue that the Scary Scooby puppet left behind.

1. WANGLEROUNDER

__ __ N __   __ __ __ __ E __ __ __ __
12   17   2   9

2. LIKESSOP   __ K __   S __ __ __ __
                               13   15

3. TEARSEW   __ W __ __ __ __ R
                     11   4   18

4. PACERFILE

    F __ __ __ P __ __ __ __
                        1   8

5. ACINGKITES

__ C __   __ K __ __ __ N __
   3   16   5   14

6. WORMSNOTS

__ __ O W __ __ __ __ M
  7   10   6

Clue #1 is:

__ __ __ __ __ __ __
1   2   3   4   5   6   7

__ __ __ __ __ __ __
8   9   10   11   12   13   14

__ __ __ __
15   16   17   18

Finding the page from the auction catalog was a good start, but we knew we had a lot more work to do. But we also knew that having Scooby walking around would be a distraction. That's why we wanted him and Shaggy to stay in the room. Of course, nothing is ever simple with the two of them. Read on to discover what kind of adventure Shaggy and Scooby had on their way back to the room.

From the desk of
Mystery, Inc.

Fred and Daphne went back to the theater to poke around for more clues, and I caught up with Shaggy and Scooby on the way back to our room. About halfway down the hallway, Scooby's nose twitched. He smelled something.

"S'mores!" Scooby said. Shaggy lifted his nose and took a deep breath.

"I'm with ya, Scoob," Shaggy said. "Let's go!"

Scooby and Shaggy took off down the hallway. I had to run to keep up. The scent led us around several bends, down a flight of stairs, and into a cold room with rows of pipes running every which way along the ceiling.

"This doesn't look like a s'mores-making machine to me," Shaggy said.

"That's because it's one of the snow feeder transfer points," a familiar voice said. Hun Strelbing stepped out from the shadows.

Not a S'mores machine

She told us how we were standing right below the indoor snowboard park. The pipes over-head carried the water used to make the ice and snow for the half-pipes and jumps. Then she asked what we were doing down there. I was about to say something when Shaggy explained that he and Scooby smelled the s'mores.

Hun looked at them skeptically. "Really?" she said. "Because it seems to me that you're really looking for a place to hide, considering your dog is a prime suspect in the diamond's disappearance."

"But it was that puppet dog that did it!" Shaggy protested.

It was clear from Hun's expression that she did not believe Shaggy.

"I've got half a mind to lock you up," Hun said. "But at least I know you can't leave the resort, what with the blizzard brewing. I'll get my proof, and when I do, you'll be sorry."

Hun turned and left, going out the same way we came in.

"Man is she scary or what?" Shaggy asked. Scooby didn't answer because his nose had picked up the s'mores trail again. We followed him up another flight of stairs

Entry #6

that led up to the snowboard park. We climbed up the circular steps and came out in a giant building. It was the size of an airplane hangar and filled with a variety of half-pipes, jumps, and other snowboarding apparatuses. And on the icy ground beside a rack of snowboards Shaggy and Scooby saw a big plate of s'mores.

"Jinkies!" I gasped. "There really were s'mores." I must admit I was totally surprised.

"See, Velma?" Shaggy said. "The nose knows!"

"Not that I want to put a damper on your fun," I said, "but why would someone leave them out here in the middle of the snowboard park?"

Scooby shrugged, then looked to see if anyone was around. He sauntered over to grab a s'more. And when he did, something burst out from behind the rack of snowboards. It was the Scooby-Doo look-alike marionette!

"Rotcha!" it shouted as it grabbed Scooby-Doo's tail.

"Raggy!" Scooby cried.

"Zoinks!" Shaggy exclaimed.

"You're coming with me!" the puppet Scooby shouted.

Rotcha!

"Oh, no he's not!" Fred yelled. That's when Fred and Daphne ran into the snowboard park. The puppet Scooby let go, grabbed a snowboard from a rack, and took off down one of the half-pipes. Though it was a little shaky at first, the marionette picked up speed and was gone by the time the rest of us got over to Scooby.

"Are you okay, Scooby?" I asked.

Scooby-Doo nodded his head.

"Reah," he said.

"I can't believe that mean marionette would do something like that," Daphne said.

"Me, neither," Shaggy added. "I mean, look, he just up and left a whole plate of s'mores here!"

"Shaggy, I was talking about how he tried to dognap Scooby," Daphne said.

"Oh, yeah," Shaggy nodded. "That, too. Now how about one of those s'mores, Scoob?"

Fred and I noticed something in the snow by the snowboard rack. Fred picked it up, and we examined it.

"That plate of s'mores wasn't the only thing the Scooby puppet left behind," Fred said. "Check this out." Fred showed us what he and Daphne had found.

If you solve the puzzle on the next page, you'll see what Fred found too!

Puzzle #6

Put the answers to the clues below in their numbered squares. When you've got all the words, unscramble the shaded letters to spell out the last clue.

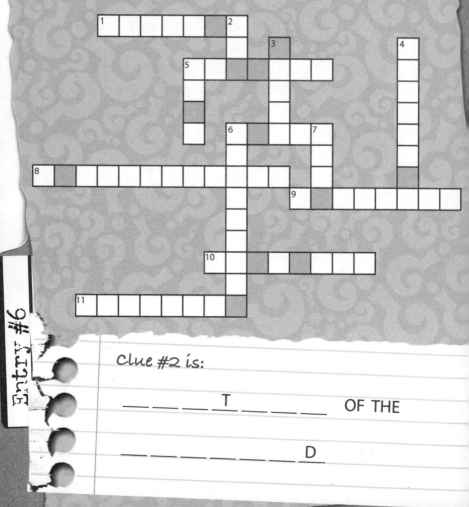

Entry #6

Clue #2 is:

___ ___ ___ T ___ ___ ___ ___ ___ OF THE

___ ___ ___ ___ ___ ___ ___ ___ D

Across

1. Wear these on your hands to keep them warm
5. This is like a hat, but it covers your whole face (except for your eyes and mouth)
6. Tie this around your neck to keep toasty
8. For an extra sweet treat, put these in the answer to #4 DOWN
9. _____ has only 28 days during a leap year
10. If you don't feel like wearing a hat, these will keep your ears warm
11. A big snowstorm

Down

2. Do this down hill or cross country
3. Wear this type of jacket, sometimes filled with down feathers
4. After hitting the slopes, warm up with a cup of this yummy drink
5. Put a snow_____ on over your clothes to stay dry in a snowball fight
6. This is like a skateboard, but for snow
7. When it's cold out, light one of these in the _____ place

The photograph of the Blizzard Diamond is one more piece of evidence to add to your collection. Once we found that, we knew that things were slowly coming together for us. But there was still more work to do. Read the next Case Files Entry to see how we worked that out.

From the desk of
Mystery, Inc.

We started to examine the photo of the Blizzard Diamond that we had just found. It showed the diamond necklace around Bridget LaNeige's neck. It was printed out on a regular piece of paper and looked sort of pixilated, like it was taken with a digital camera.

"Bridget's wearing a red, white, and blue tracksuit in this photo," Daphne said. That's when I remembered Bridget had been wearing that same outfit earlier that afternoon.

"Jeepers!" Daphne exclaimed. "That's a really important clue. Whoever this picture belongs to, they must have had a digital camera, and also a printer to print

The Blizzard
Diamond around
Bridget's neck

it out." Two people we had met earlier told us that they had a digital camera and a printer — Gordon Ticktockery and Wellington Jeffries.

"You think that's something?" Shaggy asked, interrupting my thoughts. "That crazy bodyguard of hers is ready to throw Scooby here into the hoosegow, the slammer, the big house, the pokey."

Scooby looked at Shaggy with a puzzled expression.

"Hun?" he said.

"Shaggy means that Hun Strelbing wants to send you to jail," Fred said. "Which is all the more reason to solve this case. Let's go, gang, we're running out of time!"

Fred, Daphne, and I realized that we still needed at least one more clue to solve the mystery. We decided to split up to save time.

Fred and Daphne each grabbed a snowboard and took off down the half-pipe. I told Shaggy and Scooby to follow me back into the resort building. From the snowboard park, we walked down the hallway toward the main lobby. As we walked, I noticed how people kept staring at Scooby-Doo. We overheard one of them say ". . . and it's so lifelike, too. You can't even see the seams or strings."

That gave me an idea.

"Keep your eyes peeled for a house phone," I said to Shaggy and Scooby. Sure enough, at the end of the hallway, I found one. I picked it up and asked to be connected to Mr. Pegetto's room. When he answered, I explained who I was and asked if I could meet him in his workshop.

"We're going back to the place where this whole mess started," I told Shaggy and Scooby.

"You mean the mailbox by Fred's house where he got the brochure that gave him the idea to come to the Winterama Sports Resort?" asked Shaggy.

"No, Shaggy, Paolo Pegetto's workshop where he made the Scooby marionette," I replied. I led Shaggy and Scooby through the maze of hallways and stopped when we got to the back door of the theater. I knocked, and Mr. Pegetto invited us in.

Mr. Pegetto's "workshop" was really just the backstage area, hidden behind a tall black curtain that separated it from the front of the stage. I noticed a couple of long tables with bolts of fabric and bins of beads, pins, sequins, and other sewing notions. At one end I saw a sewing machine. Several spools of very fine string stood next to it on the table.

"So what news do you have for me?" asked Paolo Pegetto.

"Only that your runaway puppet not only stole the diamond but also tried to kidnap Scooby," I said.

"Marionette," Paolo Pegetto said, correcting me. "It is a marionette, with strings from above. Not a sock with buttons for eyes. A marionette."

I apologized and asked Mr. Pegetto to explain to me how he made it. Usually he made the marionettes with sturdy inner frames. But since the Scooby marionette was made so quickly, it was a simple papier mâché shell with fabric stitched to it. In other words, it was hollow.

As I continued to look around, I asked, "And where did you leave it when you finished?"

"Over there," he answered, pointing to a rack against the back wall. The rack was right next to the door.

"So that explains how someone could have gotten in," I said. "Scooby, come over here and sit next to this rack. I want to see something."

I hoped to get an idea of exactly how the marionette was positioned. But as Scooby got to the rack, he winced in pain.

"Rikes!" he barked, pulling his front right paw off the floor.

"Like, what is it, Scoob?" asked Shaggy.

Ouch! Scooby finds a clue!

"Ri dunno," Scooby whimpered. I looked at his paw and saw something sticking in it. "It's just a pin," I said, removing it carefully. "Here you go, Mr. Pegetto." I handed it to the puppeteer and gave Scooby a pat on the head.

"This is not a pin," Paolo Pegetto said. "This is not a pin at all."

I went over for a closer look. The object was small and sharp but had a disc on one end. Instead of being flat and smooth like a straight pin, the disc was a little thicker and grooved all the way around.

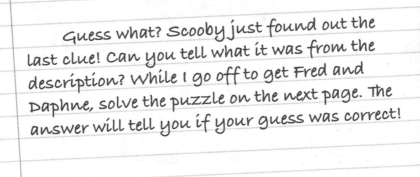

Guess what? Scooby just found out the last clue! Can you tell what it was from the description? While I go off to get Fred and Daphne, solve the puzzle on the next page. The answer will tell you if your guess was correct!

Puzzle #7

Fill in the grid with the letters below. Each letter is stacked underneath its correct column, but not in the correct row. When you're done, do what the message says and you'll find the last clue.

	O				N				H		
	L						L	U			
U		C			B	L					
	E			E	R					T	H	E
		A		E			O			

```
    S       S   I               T
  N H A       A   S
      T   F           C     N  E  E  H
  L S     R       M       I     X  T  S
  T T     D   T   D   D   B  E     E     E
```

Clue #3 is:

W _ _ _ _ _

W _ _ _ _ _ _ _ G

_ _ E _ _

Good job! You found the watch winding stem! A good detective takes his or her time to sift through all of the information that's been collected on a case. While you think about the people and clues you discovered, check out how we planned to bring Scooby's evil puppet twin to justice.

From the desk of
Mystery, Inc.

When I got back to Mr. Pegetto's workshop with Fred and Daphne, I showed them what Scooby had found. They both agreed that it was time to set a trap. And we were going to need Mr. Pegetto's help to do it. He readily agreed, but when we turned to Scooby, Shaggy stepped in.

"Man, hasn't poor Scooby-Doo here suffered enough?" asked Shaggy. "I mean, just look at him! The poor guy's been stared at, laughed at, threatened, not to mention almost kidnapped by his evil twin!"

"Nice try, Shaggy," Fred said.

"We know you've been through a lot, Scooby," Daphne said. "So how about a Scooby Snack?"

"Ror two?" Scooby asked.

"Or two," Daphne laughed. She took a couple of snacks from her bag and tossed them into the air. Scooby opened his mouth and felt them drop right in. He gobbled them down and smiled.

"Rokay, ret's go!" he barked.

I asked Mr. Pegetto to get his marionettes ready for another performance, but this time with a new cast member: Scooby-Doo.

"Huh?" he asked.

"In order to lure back the evil Scooby, we're going to reenact the crime," I explained.

"And when the puppet shows up, we'll be ready," Fred said.

"We?" asked Shaggy.

"Yes, Shaggy, you and I will be hiding behind Mr. Pegetto's curtain," Fred continued. "So when the evil Scooby shows up, we'll jump out and grab him."

But to make it authentic, there was one more person whose help we would need, so I left on my secret errand. Daphne went to gather an audience and to get Bridget LaNeige to introduce the new show. Fred found some rope backstage that he and Shaggy could use to tie up the villain once they captured him. And Shaggy helped Mr. Pegetto get the real Scooby ready by attaching some of the marionette strings to Scooby's collar and paws.

When we all came back, Daphne escorted a small crowd into the theater with Bridget LaNeige bringing up the rear. Shaggy and

Fred hid behind Mr. Pegetto's curtain, and Scooby took his place onstage alongside the other marionettes.

The houselights dimmed, and Bridget LaNeige stepped onto the stage. Shaggy peeked around the curtain and saw something dangling around her neck.

"Like, she's wearing the Blizzard Diamond!" he gasped.

She welcomed everyone back and explained that the earlier performance was entirely scripted. She told the audience that the extraordinary dog marionette coming to life and taking her necklace was all part of the show. She pointed to the Blizzard Diamond around her neck and told everyone that the earlier jewel was a replica for the show. As the crowd began to clap, Bridget introduced Paolo Pegetto once again.

Paolo Pegetto pulled on one of the real Scooby's strings, and Scooby waved at the audience. The people laughed and then cheered as suddenly another puppet stepped onto the stage. It was the other Scooby marionette. Mr. Pegetto saw it and whispered down to Fred and Shaggy.

"Now, Shaggy!" Fred yelled. He and Shaggy jumped out from behind the curtain. The

One Scooby
too many!

scary Scooby puppet saw them coming and dove headlong into the marionette stage like a football player crashing through a tackle. Fred and Shaggy fell over each other and nearly tumbled off the big stage. The scary Scooby marionette got tangled in the real Scooby's strings. They rolled head over tail across the stage. When they got to their feet, all the strings were broken. And now there was no telling them apart.

One of the Scoobys lunged forward and grabbed Bridget LaNeige's necklace and then took off out of the theater. The other Scooby growled and ran after him. The rest of us jumped up and followed the two Scoobys through the resort. The chase took us through the resort's twisting hallways and ended at the indoor snowboard park. The first Scooby grabbed a board and sailed off through the combination of icy ramps and pipes. The second Scooby took off after the first. Neither of the Scoobys was very good, but they both managed to stay upright. The final ramp lifted them into the air and onto the snowy hill at the far end of the hangar. By the time we got there, they were both lying in a snowy heap.

"How are we going to tell them apart?"
Daphne asked.

"Like, no problem, Daphne," Shaggy said.
"Hey! Who wants a Scooby Snack?"

Both Scoobys perked up and nodded their
heads excitedly.

"Now what?" asked Fred.

"Let 'em have it!" Shaggy said.

Daphne and I each threw a Scooby Snack into

the air. Both Scoobys jumped up and each gobbled one down. But one of the Scoobys hit the snow happily, while the other one started coughing.

"Uch! Ptew! Gross!" it yelled. "What is that thing?"

"Scooby-Doo, it's the end of your stealing spree!" Bridget LaNeige said as she snowboarded over to us.

Pretty exciting, huh? Believe us, we weren't sure what was going to happen at first, but things worked out just fine in the end. After she got there, Bridget LaNeige got ready to unmask the thieving Scooby marionette. But before we share with you what happened, here's your chance to put all of your hard work to the test. Follow the instructions on the next page to fill in the chart. It'll help you put all of your evidence in order so you can figure out who's behind the case of the evil puppet.

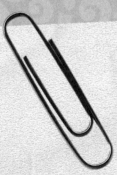

Solve the Mystery

Take the clues and suspects that you found
by solving the puzzles, and write them in their
numbered places in the chart.

Entry #8

CLUES	SUSPECTS		
Write the clue from each of the puzzles:	Write the name of the suspect from each of the puzzles:		
	Suspect #1 is: _____	Suspect #2 is: _____	Suspect #3 is: _____
Clue #1 is: _____			
Clue #2 is: _____			
Clue #3 is: _____			

◎ If a suspect can be connected to a clue, mark the box where the suspect column meets the clue row with an X.

◎ When you're done, there should be only one suspect with three X's in their column.

◎ Write that suspect's name here: _____

When you think you know who's behind the mystery, turn the page to see what happened when we unmasked the scary Scooby puppet!

A small crowd had gathered at the bottom of the snowy hill. Shaggy helped the real Scooby up and stood by his friend. The rest of us watched as Bridget LaNeige approached the phony Scooby and reached down to pull off its mask. She gave a tug, but it wouldn't budge.

"The stitching is too strong," Paolo Pegetto said as he stepped through the crowd. He removed a small pair of scissors from his hip-pack and carefully cut along the collar line. He stepped away to allow Bridget to unmask the villain. She reached down and gave a swift yank. Bridget gasped.

"Who are you?" she asked. She took a closer look at the bushy mustache and sweaty face of the man in the Scooby costume. "Wait, you do look familiar to me. Where have I seen you before?"

"Maybe this will help remind you," Daphne said. She handed Bridget the Blizzard

It was Gordon
Ticktockery!

Diamond page from the Anne Tique's Auction House booklet. Bridget's eyes lit up.

"Of course!" she said. "You're that man who bid against me for the Blizzard Diamond!"

"Really? You did?" asked Bridget. "But why?"

Fred stepped forward to say, "Well, it wasn't easy, but we collected a series of clues that led us to that conclusion. For instance, the piece of paper you're holding in your hand."

Bridget LaNeige looked down at the page from the auction catalog. Daphne told her it was the first thing the Scooby marionette dropped after stealing the Blizzard Diamond. Daphne mentioned that we had met three different people, all of whom said they were at the auction. One of them was Gordon Ticktockery.

"And so was I," Wellington Jeffries said as he stepped from the crowd. "I was there because I was hoping to get the diamond back into my family. I've been trying to talk to you for a long time, but your bodyguard kept me away."

"Just doing my job," Hun Strelbing replied.

Entry #9

I started to add that Hun was another suspect, and that's when she cut me off.

"It's true, Bridge," she said. "I've been a little jealous ever since you took my slot at the Olympics. But believe me, I would never do something like this."

"I believe you," Bridget said.

And with that Fred showed Bridget the second clue we found: the photograph of her wearing the diamond. It had been taken with a digital camera, and a lot of people travel with those, but not many people bring their printers with them like Gordon Ticktockery and Wellington Jeffries said they had. Daphne reassured Bridget that when we found the second clue, we knew that Hun couldn't be a suspect any longer.

Then I explained how it was the last clue that tipped us off to the villain's true identity. I held out the pin that wasn't really a pin. It was the winding stem from an old fashioned wristwatch.

"And we remembered that Mr. Ticktockery had showed us an antique watch whose winding stem kept falling off," Daphne said. "That's what clinched it for us."

Bridget looked at Gordon Ticktockery. "You know, I felt so bad about beating you at the auction," she said. "That's why I told my staff to give you extra snowboarding lessons. Little did I know what you would do with them! But why would you go through all this trouble?"

"Because you humiliated me in front of my colleagues!" Gordon whined. "I've never lost at an auction before, and once you beat me, my reputation was ruined! I can never go to another auction again! And it's all because of you, you and those meddling kids and their pesky pooch!"

"Come with me Mr. Ticktockery," Hun Strelbing said. "I'm going to guard you myself until the police arrive."

"Just one moment, Ms. Strelbing," Fred said. "I believe he has something that belongs to Ms. LaNeige."

Gordon Ticktockery reached into the costume and took out the Blizzard Diamond. He tossed it to Bridget and sneered, "It's just the fake. That dog took the real one from you."

"I'm afraid not," I said. "The one that Scooby-Doo took a few minutes ago was the replica that Wellington Jeffries created. You had the real one in your hands all along, Mr. Ticktockery."

Scooby took the fake diamond out from under his collar. Gordon Ticktockery's face turned white. He was so angry all he could do was spit and stammer as Hun Strelbing led him away.

Bridget took the replica from Scooby and took some folded papers from her pocket. She turned to Wellington Jeffries and told him that one of her employees found his papers on the ground. Bridget offered to meet with Wellington Jeffries to discuss the rightful ownership of the Blizzard Diamond. Then she thanked us.

"We were glad to help, Ms. LaNeige," Fred said. "You really don't have to do anything."

Scooby whispered something to Shaggy, who whispered something to Bridget, who smiled.

Soon, we were all warm and cozy in the resort's lobby sipping hot chocolate. Shaggy and Scooby sat happily around the lobby fireplace, roasting marshmallows.

"Shkooby Dooby Doooo!" Scooby cheered through a mouthful of gooey s'mores.

Congratulations . . . you did it! We think you've got what it takes to be an honorary member of Mystery, Inc! So be on the lookout for more Scooby-Doo Case Files! We'll be glad to have you come along and help solve another mystery with me, Fred, Daphne, Shaggy, and of course, Scooby-Doo!

Puzzle #1 — Pg. 11

A DOUGHNUT

Puzzle #2 — Pg. 20

| E | L | M | A | B | C | D | F | G | H | I | J | K | N | O | P | Q | R | S | T | U | W | X | Y | Z |
| B | C | D | E | F | G | H | I | J | K | L | M | N | O | P | Q | R | S | T | U | V | W | X | Y | Z |

Suspect #1 is: HUN STRELBING
The motive is: She lost the gold medal to Bridget!

Puzzle #3 — Pg. 29

REACHES and RESEA**R**CH
NO**O**DLE and OLDEN
REPEAT and **O**PERATE
WINGED and WE**D**DING
TRA**C**ING and RATING
SP**O**OLS and SLOPS
PLA**T**TERS and STAPLER
NOTE and TO**K**EN
FRIED and F**I**NDER
SE**C**RET and RESET
SHOT and **G**HOST
WOND**E**R and DROWN
WRI**T**ING and WIRING
PERCH and **C**IPHER
SEA and EAS**Y**

Suspect #2: GORDON TICKTOCKERY

Puzzle #4 — Pg. 37

Suspect #3: WELLINGTON JEFFRIES

Puzzle #5 — Pg. 44

Solution:
1. LONG UNDERWEAR 4. FIREPLACE
2. SKI SLOPE 5. ICE SKATING
3. SWEATER 6. SNOWSTORM

Clue #1: AUCTION CATALOG PAGE

Puzzle #6 — Pg. 52

Clue #2 is a: PICTURE OF THE DIAMOND

Puzzle #7 — Pg. 61

TO FIND THE
LAST CLUE
UNSCRAMBLE THE
LETTERS IN THE
SHADED BOXES

Clue #3: WATCH WINDING STEM

Solve the Mystery — Pg. 71

CLUES Write the clue from each of the puzzles:	SUSPECTS Write the name of the suspect from each of the puzzles:		
	Suspect #1 is: Hun Strelbing	Suspect #2 is: Gordon Ticktockery	Suspect #3 is: Wellington Jeffries
Auction Clue #1 is: catalog page	X	X	X
Picture of the Clue #2 is: diamond		X	X
Watch winding Clue #3 is: stem			X